Cat Club

Birmans

by Cameron L. Woodson

Bullfrog Books

Ideas for Parents and Teachers

Bullfrog Books let children practice reading informational text at the earliest reading levels. Repetition, familiar words, and photo labels support early readers.

Before Reading

- Discuss the cover photo. What does it tell them?
- Look at the picture glossary together. Read and discuss the words.

Read the Book

- "Walk" through the book and look at the photos. Let the child ask questions. Point out the photo labels.
- Read the book to the child, or have him or her read independently.

After Reading

- Prompt the child to think more. Ask: Birmans have a special color pattern. Can you think of other cats that have a special color pattern?

Bullfrog Books are published by Jump!
5357 Penn Avenue South
Minneapolis, MN 55419
www.jumplibrary.com

Library of Congress Cataloging-in-Publication Data

Names: Woodson, Cameron L., 1994– author.
Title: Birmans / Cameron L. Woodson.
Description: Minneapolis: Jump!, Inc., [2021]
Series: Cat club | Includes index.
Audience: Ages 5–8 | Audience: Grades K–1
Identifiers: LCCN 2019049077 (print)
LCCN 2019049078 (ebook)
ISBN 9781645274476 (hardcover)
ISBN 9781645274483 (ebook)
Subjects: LCSH: Birman cat—Juvenile literature.
Classification: LCC SF449.B5 W66 2021 (print)
LCC SF449.B5 (ebook)
DDC 636.8/24—dc23
LC record available at https://lccn.loc.gov/2019049077
LC ebook record available at
https://lccn.loc.gov/2019049078

Editors: Jenna Gleisner and Susanne Bushman
Designer: Jenna Casura

Photo Credits: Eric Isselee/Shutterstock, cover, 1, 3, 8–9 (foreground), 23br, 24; Borkin Vadim/Shutterstock, 4, 10, 20–21, 23tl; Jean-Michel Labat/Pantheon/SuperStock, 5 (foreground); Yuganov Konstantin/Shutterstock, 5 (background); Juhku/Shutterstock, 6–7; jhorrocks/iStock, 8–9 (background), 23br; blickwinkel/Alamy, 11, 23bl; GlobalP/iStock, 12–13 (foreground), 18–19 (cat), 22, 23tr; Rawpixel/iStock, 12–13 (background); Petra Wegner/Alamy, 14–15; Tierfotoagentur/Alamy, 16; Juniors Bildarchiv GmbH/Alamy, 17; LightFieldStudios/iStock, 18–19 (child), 23tr.

Printed in the United States of America at Corporate Graphics in North Mankato, Minnesota.

Table of Contents

Playful Pals

This is a Birman!

These cats are friendly.
They love other pets.

kittens

Birmans are born all white.

ruff

They grow.
Their fur is long.
It is mostly white.
Look! It has a ruff.

Its tail is bushy.
It is dark.

So is its face and ears.
We call this a point pattern.

Their legs are darker, too.

But their paws are white!

Cute!

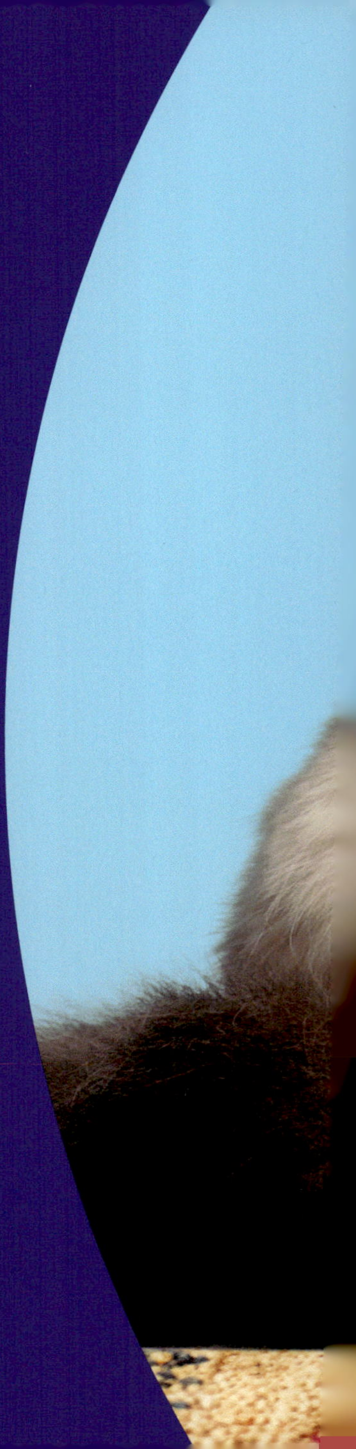

paw

All Birmans have blue eyes.

Pretty!

They love to play!

We play every day!

They are curious.

Mine wants to help with chores!

Do you want a Birman?

A Birman Up Close

A Birman has long, white fur. It has a bushy tail and a ruff. Look at its other body parts!

Picture Glossary

bushy
Thick and spreading.

curious
Eager to know or learn about something.

point pattern
A color pattern in which fur on the face, tail, legs, and ears is darker.

ruff
A collar of fur.

Index

To Learn More

Finding more information is as easy as 1, 2, 3.

1. Go to www.factsurfer.com
2. Enter "Birmans" into the search box.
3. Click the "Surf" button to see a list of websites.